**M. P. Robertson** studied Graphic Design at Kingston University.
Since 1988 he has been a freelance illustrator specialising in children's books.
Among his previous titles are *Grizelda Frizzle* with Brian Patten,
*The Bed and Breakfast House* with Tony Barton, *A Very Smelly History*
with Mary Dobson, and *The Thwarting of Baron Bolligrew* with Robert Bolt.
*Seven Ways to Catch the Moon* is his first book for Frances Lincoln.
M. P. Robertson lives in Wiltshire with his partner and
two young children.

For my dad who drew me pictures,
and my mum who put everything in plastic bags.

*Seven Ways to Catch the Moon* copyright © Frances Lincoln Limited 1999
Text and illustrations copyright © M. P. Robertson 1999

First published in Great Britain in 1999 by
Frances Lincoln Limited, 4 Torriano Mews
Torriano Avenue, London NW5 2RZ

First paperback edition 2000

British Library Cataloguing in Publication Data
available on request

ISBN 0-7112-1412-3 hardback
ISBN 0-7112-1413-1 paperback

Set in Myriad Tilt

Printed in Hong Kong

1 3 5 7 9 8 6 4 2

# SEVEN WAYS TO CATCH
# THE MOON

## M. P. Robertson

FRANCES LINCOLN

There are seven ways
to catch the moon.

The first is to float in a hot air balloon...

but beware the point of the crescent moon.

The second is to ride on a shooting star...

but be careful not to shoot too far.

The third is to build a pair of wings...

but only use the strongest strings.

The fourth is to hi

ith a moon-struck witch...

but the witch's broom gives a sudden twitch.

The fifth is to climb on a dragon's back...

but mind you don't become his snack.

The seventh way
is to close your eyes,
and dream a dream
of midnight skies.